ILLUSTRATED CLASSICS

The Railway
Children

by
Edith Nesbit

Adapted by
Bookmatrix Ltd

Edited by
Claire Black

Published by

Berryland
Books
www.berrylandbooks.com

The Railway Children

by
Edith Nesbit

First Published in 2006 • Copyright © Berryland Books 2006
ISBN 1-84577-593-7 • Printed in India

Contents

CHAPTER I

The Beginning

Roberta, Peter and Phyllis were not really railway children; they were just ordinary suburban children, who lived in a common red, brick-fronted villa. The only time that they had anything to do with a train was when the family went out of the city for their vacations.

Roberta, whose pet name was Bobbie, was the eldest of all of them. Of course, mothers never have favorites, but if the children's mother did have a favorite, it would have been Roberta. Next came Peter, who wished to be an engineer when he grew up; and the youngest was Phyllis.

These children were lucky to have everything they ever needed—pretty clothes, good fires and a lovely nursery with heaps of toys. They had a dog, which actually was their own, and they called him James. They also had a father who was just perfect—never cross, never unjust, and always ready to play with them. Their mother spent most of her time playing with the children and helping out with their home lessons, unlike other mothers, who loved to spend time with their own friends. Besides, she wrote interesting stories for them while they were at school, and read them aloud after tea. She also made up funny poems for their birthdays and other 'great' occasions, such as the christening of the new kittens, or the refurnishing o peared.

"What would you like to have?" she asked.

"Pigeon pie," Peter said, eagerly, "a very large pigeon pie."

And so a large pigeon pie was made for Peter and he ate it.

None of them was able to fix up Peter's engine. The only person they believed could do so was father. But father had been away in the country for three or four days. They waited till evening, for father would be back by then. Father could mend all sorts of things. He had often acted as veterinary surgeon to their wooden rocking horse, and once he had saved its life when even the carpenter had given up.

Mother had told Peter that it would be a good idea to be unselfish and not tell father about the problem till he was rested. So Peter waited patiently till father had finished dinner.

At last mother said to father, "Now, dear, we want to tell you about the great railway accident, and ask your advice."

"All right," said father, "fire away!"

So Peter narrated the sad tale, and fetched what was left of the engine.

"Hmm!" said father, when he had looked at the damaged engine carefully.

The children held their breath.

"Is there any hope?" Peter asked in a low and trembling voice.

"Hope? Of course there is. And a lot of hope indeed," said father, cheerfully. "All it needs is some solder, and a new valve. Let's keep it for Saturday when all of you can help me."

Just then there was a knock at the front door. Ruth, the parlor maid came in to say that two gentlemen wanted to see the master.

"I've shown them into the library, sir," she said.

"Do hurry back, dear," mother whispered as he went towards the library.

However this was not to be. As the wait became longer and longer, mother tried to make the time pass by telling the children a new fairy story. For once, though, she could not hold their attention. Loud voices came through the library door and father's voice came across the loudest. Then the bell rang, and everyone heaved a sigh of relief.

"They're going now," Phyllis said.

But instead, Ruth came in. She seemed agitated.

"Please ma'am," she said, "the master wants you to come into the study. He is looking pale; I think he's had some bad news."

"That'll do, Ruth," mother said gently, "you can go."

Mother went into the library, and there was more talking. Then the bell rang again and Ruth was asked to fetch a cab. The children heard people walk out and the cab drive away. They sensed that all was not well as they heard the front door shut, and mother walked in—her face as white as a sheet; her eyes large and shining.

"It's bedtime," she said, her voice barely above a whisper. "Ruth will put you to bed."

"But you promised we would sit up late tonight because father has come home," Phyllis said.

"Father's been called away on business," mother said. "Come, darlings, go at once."

They kissed her and left.

Roberta gave her mother an extra hug and whispered, "It wasn't bad news, mummy, was it?"

"I can't tell you anything tonight, my pet. Go, dear, go now."

So Roberta too left along with Phyllis and Peter.

Late that night, mother came up and kissed all three children as they lay asleep. Roberta was the only one who woke up with the kiss, but she lay as still as a mouse and said nothing.

'If mother doesn't want us to know she's been

crying,' she told herself as she heard her mother weep, 'we *won't* know it. That's all.'

When they came down to breakfast the next morning, mother had already gone out.

"Where has mother gone?" Phyllis asked.

"To London," Ruth said abruptly.

"Something awful must have happened," Peter said—more to himself than to others while breaking his egg.

Quietly, they had their breakfast and left for school. Mother was still not home when they returned at one o'clock for lunch. Nor was she there at teatime either. It was nearly seven when she came in and sank into an armchair. She looked so ill and tired that the children felt they should not ask her any questions.

After a cup of tea, mother said, "Now, my darlings, I want to tell you something. Those men, last night, did bring very bad news, and father will be away for some time. I am very worried. I want you all to help me and not make things more difficult. You can do so in a big way by being good and not quarrelling whenever I'm away."

"We won't quarrel," chorused all three together.

And that day, for once, when Roberta, Peter and Phyllis said it, they meant it too.

"Then," mother went on, "I want you not to ask me any questions about this trouble."

After a pause, she continued, "It isn't necessary for you to know anything about it, as it is related to business, and you do not understand business, do you?"

"No. Is it something to do with the government?" asked Roberta, for father was in a government office.

"Yes," mother said. "Now it's bedtime, my darlings. And don't you worry. It's going to be all right in the end."

"Then you don't worry either, mother," Phyllis said, "and we'll all be as good as gold."

Mother sighed and kissed them good night.

"I say," Phyllis said, once they were alone, "you used to say it was so dull, nothing happening, like in books. Now something has happened."

"But I never wanted things to happen to make mother unhappy," Roberta said sadly.

CHAPTER 2

A New House

Everything continued to be perfectly horrid for some weeks. Mother was always out and mealtimes were dull. To make matters worse, Aunt Emma came on a visit. She was much older than mother and believed in keeping children in their proper places. And they more than returned the compliment. Their idea of Aunt Emma's proper place was anywhere where they could see as little of her as possible.

They preferred the company of the servants, who were more amusing. However, the servants never told the children what bad news the gentlemen had brought with them.

Then one day, mother came home and went straight to bed. There she stayed for two days. The doctor came, and the children crept miserably about the house and wondered if the world was coming to an end. But then on the third day morning, mother came down to breakfast. She appeared very pale and there were lines on her face.

She gave a weak smile and said, "Now, my pets, everything is settled. We're going to leave this house, and go and live in a beautiful little white house in the country. I know you'll love it."

This announcement was followed by packing—not just clothes-as you do when you go to the seaside but furniture, books, boxes and all sorts of things. The children enjoyed it very much. All their beds had gone. A bed was made up for Peter on the drawing room sofa.

"I say, this is great," he said, tossing and turning joyously, as mother tucked him up. "I do like moving! I wish we moved once a month."

"I don't!" she laughed.

"Good night, Peterkin."

As she turned away, Roberta saw her face. She never forgot it.

'Oh, mother!' she whispered to herself as she got into bed. 'How brave you are! You are being brave enough to laugh when you're feeling so low. I love you so much!'

The next day lots and lots of boxes were filled. Then late in the afternoon, a cab came to take them to the station. Aunt Emma saw them off. At first they enjoyed looking out of the window, but as evening descended, they grew more and more sleepy. None of them knew how long they had been in the train, when mother woke them up to say that their station had arrived. They stood around—cold and melancholy—shivering on the draughty platform, while the baggage was being taken out of the train and loaded onto a cart. They watched miserably as the engine pulled out puffing and blowing, till it disappeared into the darkness.

This was the first time that they saw the railway which was soon to become the center of their lives. They shivered and sneezed and hoped that the walk to the new house would not be long. Peter's nose was colder than ever and Phyllis' shoelaces had come undone as usual.

"Come," mother said, "we've got to walk. There aren't any cabs here."

The walk was dark and muddy. The children stumbled a little on the rough road, and Phyllis absent-mindedly fell into a puddle. She was picked up damp and unhappy.

"There's the house," mother said. "I wonder why she's shut the windows!"

"Who's *she*?" asked Roberta.

"The woman I engaged to clean the place, and put the furniture straight and get supper."

There was a low wall, and trees inside.

"That's the garden," mother said.

There was no light in any of the windows. Everyone hammered at the door, but no one answered.

The man who drove their cart said, "You see, your train was late, so she must have left for home."

"But she's got the key," mother said.

"Oh, she might have left that under the doorstep," said the cart-man, "as the people here normally do."

He took the lantern off his cart and stooped.

"Yes, here it is," he said and unlocked the door with it.

He set the lantern on the table.

"Do you know where we can find a candle?" he asked.

"I don't know where anything is," mother replied quite cheerlessly.

The cart-man struck a match and lighted a candle, which he found on the table. By its thin little glimmer, the children saw a large bare kitchen with a stone floor. The kitchen table from home stood in the middle of the room, and the chairs were placed in one corner. The pots, pans, brooms, and crockery were stacked up in another. There was no fire. Only cold, dead ashes in the fireplace! As the cart-man turned to go out after he had brought in the boxes, there was a rustling sound that seemed to come from inside the walls of the house.

"Oh, what's that?" cried the girls.

"It's only the rats," he shouted over his back as he drove away.

A sudden flow of air blew out the candle.

"Oh dear, I wish we hadn't come!" Phyllis said, as she knocked a chair over.

"Only the rats!" Peter exclaimed, in the dark.

"What fun!" mother said, in the dark, feeling for the matches on the table. She struck a match and lighted the candle and everyone looked at each other.

"You've often wanted something to happen and now it has. This is quite an adventure, isn't it? I told Mrs. Viney to have supper ready. I suppose she's laid it in the dining room. So let's go and see."

The dining room opened out of the kitchen. Sure enough, there was the table and the chairs, but where was the supper?

"Let's look in the other rooms," mother said and they trooped out to check the other rooms.

In each room, there was the same kind of half-arranged furniture but nothing to eat.

"What a horrible old woman!" mother said. "She's just walked off with the money and not got us anything to eat."

"Then are we not going to have any supper at all?" asked Phyllis, dismayed.

"Oh, yes," mother said, "only it'll mean unpacking one of those big cases."

Finally, after a lot of hitting and hammering, the box opened.

"Hurrah!" mother exclaimed. "Here are some candles! You girls go and light them."

"How many shall we light?"

"As many as you like," mother said, with a smile. "The most important thing is to be cheerful. Nobody can be cheerful in the dark except owls and dormice."

The girls lighted fourteen candles in the dining room. Roberta then went to fetch coal and wood to light a fire. The fire and candles made the dining room look a lot more cheerful, and the girls hastily 'tidied' the room.

"Bravo!" cried mother, coming in with a tray full of things. "I'll just get a tablecloth and then we can have our supper."

Mother got the tablecloth and then a real feast was laid out on it. Everyone was very, very tired, but got cheered up at the sight of the funny and delightful supper. There were biscuits—the Marie and the plain kind—sardines, preserved ginger, cooking raisins, and candied peel and marmalade.

"It's a good thing Aunt Emma packed up all the odds and ends from the store cupboard," mother said.

"Let's drink to Aunt Emma's health," Roberta said, suddenly. "What would we have done if she hadn't packed up these things? Here's to Aunt Emma!"

And they drank the ginger wine and water. They all felt that they had been a little hard on Aunt Emma. After dinner, they quickly made their beds.

"Good night," mother said. "I'm sure there aren't any rats, but I'll leave my door open. If a mouse does come, just scream. I'll come and tell it exactly what I think of it."

Mother's assurance help the children go off to sleep immediately.

The next morning, Roberta woke up Phyllis by pulling her hair gently.

"Wassermarrer?" asked Phyllis, still half asleep.

"Wake up! Wake up!" Roberta said. "We're in the new house—don't you remember? No servants or anything. Let's get up and begin to be useful. We'll make everything beautiful before mother gets up."

By the time they were dressed, Peter too was ready. Of course, there was no water in their room, so when they got down, they washed as much as they thought was necessary under the spout of the pump in the yard. One pumped and the other washed. It was splashy but interesting.

"It's much more fun than washing in a basin," remarked Roberta.

"This is far, far, far and way prettier than Edgecombe Villa," declared Phyllis. "Let's go in and begin to work."

They lighted the fire, put the kettle on, and arranged the crockery for breakfast though they could not find all the right things. After they did everything they could do, they went out again into the fresh, bright morning.

It was a hilly country. Down below, they could see the railway line and the black, yawning mouth of a tunnel. The station was out of sight. There was a great bridge with tall arches running across one end of the valley. The children sat down on a great flat gray stone that had pushed itself up out of the grass. When mother came out to look for them at eight o'clock, she found them fast asleep.

They had made an excellent fire, and had set the kettle on it at about half past five. By eight, the fire had been out for some time, the water had all boiled away, and the bottom of the kettle was burned out. But mother did not scold them as they were only trying to be helpful. She then took them to the room which they had mistaken the previous night for a cabinet. The children could not believe their eyes. Before them on a table, was a joint of cold roast beef, with bread, butter, cheese, and a pie.

"Pie for breakfast!" cried Peter.

"Well, this is the supper we ought to have had last night," mother said. "And there was a note from Mrs. Viney that her son-in-law had broken his arm, and she had to get home early. She's coming today at ten."

It was a wonderful breakfast and the children loved every bite of it.

"You see it's more like dinner than breakfast to us," Peter said, passing his plate for more, "because we were up so early."

The day passed in helping mother to unpack and arrange things. Six small legs quite ached with running about, while their owners carried clothes and crockery and all sorts of things to their proper places.

It was not till quite late in the afternoon that mother said, "There! That'll do for today."

Once mother said so, all of them had just one question.

Q. "Where do we go now?"

A. "To the railway."

And so to the railway they went.

CHAPTER 3

The Railway

On the way to the railway, they saw the garden they had seen the night before. It had a high wall all round it.

The track leading to the railway line was all

downhill. It was covered with smooth turf and strewn with gray and yellow rocks. It ended in a steep run and a wooden fence. They all climbed onto the top of the fence, and there, before them was the railway with the shining metals, the telegraph wires, the posts and signals. Suddenly there was a rumbling sound that made them look along the line to the right. The dark mouth of the tunnel yawned on the face of a rocky cliff. The next moment, a train shot out of the tunnel. Shrieking and snorting, it rumbled past them.

"Oh!" Roberta said, drawing a long breath. "It was like a great dragon rushing by. Did you feel its hot wings fan us?"

Peter said, "I never thought we would ever see a train from so near. It's the most ripping sport!"

"I wonder if that train was going to London!" Bobbie said.

"Let's go down to the station and find out," Peter said.

So they went. They walked along the edge of the line and heard the telegraph wires humming over their heads. Finally after a long walk, they reached the station. Never before had any of them been to a station, except to catch a train or receive someone, and always with grown-ups. The absence of grown-ups made a lot of difference. This in itself was a great adventure.

They peeped into the porters' room. There was a lone porter, and he was half asleep behind a paper. There were a great many lines crossing at the station, with some of them ending abruptly in a yard. Trucks stood on the rails here, and on one side of the yard was a great heap of coal. It was like a solid building built of large square blocks of coal. There was a line of whitewash near the top of the coaly wall.

The porter came out at the sound of the station gong and Peter asked him what the white mark on the coal was for.

"To mark how much coal is there, so that

we know immediately if anyone has stolen any," replied the porter.

Peter did not think about it much at that time, but it remained at the back of his mind.

The three of them walked along the lines for a while and finally came back home.

** ** ** ** ** ** ** ** ** **

Mother had been very sad ever since father went away. Though the children did not forget him, they soon got used to being without father. They got used to not going to school, and seeing very little of mother. Now she spent almost all day shut up in her room upstairs— writing, writing and writing. She just came down at teatime and read aloud the stories she had written. Gradually, the memories of their life at the villa began to fade away.

Though mother had told them more than once that they were 'quite poor now,' the children did not feel much of a difference as they still had everything they wanted. But with

June came three rainy days. It rained heavily and the weather turned very cold. They all went up to mother's room and knocked at the door.

"Well, what is it?" asked mother from inside.

"Mother," Bobbie said, "may I light a fire?"

And mother answered, "No, my dear. We mustn't have fires in June—coal is so expensive. If you are cold, go and play in the attic. That'll warm you. Now run away, I'm terribly busy!"

"Mother's always busy now," Phyllis whispered to Peter.

Peter did not answer. He shrugged his shoulders. He was thinking.

However, they all went up to the attic to play.

The same evening at tea, when Phyllis was going to add jam to her bread and butter, mother said, "Jam or butter, dear—not jam *and* butter. We can't afford that sort of reckless luxury nowadays."

Phyllis finished the slice of bread and butter

in silence, and followed it up by bread and jam.

Peter was lost in his own thoughts and after tea he told his sisters, "I have an idea."

"What's that?" they asked eagerly.

"I am not going to tell you," was Peter's unexpected reply.

"Oh, very well," Bobbie said, "I don't want to know about your silly ideas."

"You'll know some day," Peter said, trying not to lose his temper. "The only reason why I won't tell you my idea now is because it may be wrong and I don't want to drag you into it."

"Don't you do it if it's wrong, Peter," Bobbie said. "Let me do it instead of you."

But Phyllis said, "If *you* are going to do wrong, I should like to do it too!"

"No," Peter said, quite touched by this devotion. "All I request is that if mother asks where I am, you won't blab."

Two evenings after this conversation took place, Peter called the girls.

"Come with me," he said, "and bring the Roman Chariot."

The Roman Chariot was a very old perambulator that was in the loft.

"Follow your leader," Peter said and led the way down the hill.

He came to a halt after some time and said, "Here's the first coal from the 'St. Peter's Mine.' We'll take it home in the chariot."

At first, the chariot was packed full of coal. However, the children then found it too heavy to wheel it uphill, and so it had to be partially unpacked again! Finally, they had to make three journeys to add the coal from Peter's mine to mother's cellar.

The children's expedition to the coal mine continued. It was around a week later that Mrs. Viney remarked to mother how well the last lot of coal was holding out. When the children heard this, they hugged themselves and struggled hard to stop themselves from bursting into laughter.

Very soon they had all forgotten that there had ever been any doubt in Peter's mind as to whether 'coal mining' was wrong. But there came a dreadful night when the stationmaster crept out very quietly to the yard and waited like a cat by a mouse hole. He saw something small and dark scrabbling on the top of the heap. The stationmaster waited till the small thing on the top of the heap came to the edge. And then his hand fell on the small thing, and there was Peter, firmly held by the jacket. He had an old carpenter's bag full of coal in his trembling hands.

"So I've caught you at last, haven't I, you young thief?" said the stationmaster.

"I'm not a thief," Peter said, as firmly as he could. "I'm a coal-miner."

"Shut up and come along to the station."

"Oh, no," cried an agonized voice in the darkness.

"Not the *police* station!" said another voice from the darkness. "Can't you decide now what you'll do to us? It's our fault just as much as Peter's. We helped to carry the coal away and we knew where he got it."

"No, you didn't," Peter said.

"Yes, we did," Bobbie said. "We knew it all the time. We only pretended we didn't."

"Don't hold me!" Peter said. "I won't run away."

The stationmaster loosened Peter's collar, struck a match and looked at them by its flickering light.

"Why!" he exclaimed. You're the children from the Three Chimneys up there. Tell me now, what made you steal?"

"I didn't think I was stealing. If I had taken it out from the sides then it would have been stealing, but I dug it out from the middle. So I had to *mine* it," Peter said indignantly.

"But did you do it for fun?" asked the stationmaster.

"Oh, you think we would cart that heavy thing uphill for fun?" Peter asked.

"Then why *did* you?" The stationmaster's voice was much kinder now.

"You remember that rainy day?" Peter replied. "Well, that day when we were cold, mother said we were too poor to have a fire. We always had fires when it was cold at our other house, and..."

"Well," said the stationmaster, thoughtfully, "I will let you go this time but remember, stealing is stealing, whether you call it mining or whether you don't. Now run along home."

"Do you mean you aren't going to do anything to us? Well, you are a brick!" Peter said with enthusiasm.

"You're a dear!" Bobbie said.

"You're a darling!" Phyllis chipped in.

"That's all right," said the stationmaster.

And on this, they parted and ran uphill to the Three Chimneys.

CHAPTER 4

The Old Gentleman

Even after the misadventure of Peter's coal mine, the children could not keep away from the railway. They had begun to know the hours when certain trains passed, and they gave names to them. The 9.15 UP was called the 'green dragon.' The 10.07 DOWN was the 'worm of wantley.' The midnight town express, whose shrieking sometimes shattered their dreams, was the 'fearsome fly-by-night.' Peter got up once in the middle of the night, peeped through his curtains, and named it on the spot.

It was by the 'green dragon' that the old gentleman traveled. He was a very nice-looking old gentleman. He had a fresh-collar, clean-shaven face and white hair, and he wore rather odd-shaped collars and a top hat that was different from what others used. Of course, the children didn't see all this at first. In fact, the first thing they noticed about the old gentleman was his hand.

It happened one morning, as they sat on the fence waiting for the 'green dragon.' It was three and a quarter minutes late by Peter's Waterbury watch.

"The 'green dragon's' going to where father is," Phyllis said. "If it were really a real dragon, we could stop it and ask it to take our love to father. I wonder why father never writes to us."

"Mother says he's been too busy," Bobbie answered, "but he'll write soon."

"I say," Phyllis suggested, "let's all wave to the 'green dragon' as it goes by. If it's a magic dragon, it'll understand and take our love to father. And if it isn't, three waves aren't much. We shall never miss them."

So when the 'green dragon' came out of the mouth of the dark tunnel shrieking, all three children stood on the railing and waved their pocket-handkerchiefs. And out of a first—class carriage a hand with a newspaper waved back. It was the old gentleman's hand. After this it became the custom for waves to be exchanged between the children and the 9.15 train.

Mother, all this time, was very busy with her writing. She would send her stories to the editors and whenever an editor selected her story, there were buns for tea.

One day, when Peter was going down to the village to get buns for tea, he met the stationmaster. Peter felt very uncomfortable, for he had by now realized that his 'coal mining' was less of mining and more of what the stationmaster had said. He did not like to wish 'good morning' to the stationmaster. So he looked down, and said nothing.

It was the stationmaster who wished 'good morning' as he passed by.

And Peter answered, 'good morning.'

Then he thought, 'Perhaps he does not recognize me by daylight, or he would not be so polite.'

And then before he knew what he was doing, he ran up to the stationmaster and said, "I don't want you to be polite to me if you don't know who I am."

"Eh?" said the stationmaster.

"I thought perhaps you didn't know it was me who took the coals," Peter went on, "when you said 'good morning.' But it was me, and I'm sorry."

"Why," said the stationmaster, "I wasn't thinking anything at all about the precious coals. Let bygones be bygones. You may visit us at the station whenever you want."

"Thank you," Peter said, "I'm very glad that you have excused me."

The stationmaster left with this and Peter ran to get the buns, feeling more comfortable.

The next day after they had sent their wave of greeting to father by the 'green dragon,' Peter proudly led the way to the station. Bobbie and Phyllis did not want to go, but when Peter told them about his meeting with the stationmaster and his invitation, the girls readily accompanied him.

"Stop a minute, my bootlace is undone again!" cried out Phyllis on the way.

"It is always undone," Peter said.

Phyllis did up her bootlace and went on in silence.

They reached the station and spent two happy hours with the porter. They became good friends and he never seemed tired of answering their questions. He told them many things that they had not known before—for instance, the things that hook carriages together are called couplings; the pipes that hang like great serpents over the couplings are used to stop the train.

"If you can get hold of one of them when the train is going and pull them apart," he said, "she'd stop dead with a jerk."

"Who's she?" Phyllis asked.

"The train, of course," replied the porter.

After that the train was never again 'It' to the children.

The children had a delightful conversation with the porter and did not realize how the time had flown by so quickly. The stationmaster came out once or twice and was very nice to them.

"Just as if coal had never been discovered," Phyllis whispered to her sister.

He gave them each an orange, and promised to take them up into the signal-box one of these days, when he was not too busy.

That evening they went back and told mother all about the railway, the porter and the stationmaster.

"I'm so glad you like the railway. Only, please, you mustn't walk on the line."

"Mother, didn't you ever walk on the railway lines when you were little?" asked Phyllis.

"Yes, but darlings you don't know how fond I am of you. What should I do if you got hurt?"

"Are you more fond of us than granny was of you when you were little?" Phyllis asked.

Bobbie made signs to her to stop, but Phyllis never did see signs—no matter how plain they might be. Mother did not answer for a minute.

"No one," she said at last, "ever loved anyone more than my mother loved me."

Bobbie kicked Phyllis hard under the table. She

yelled, "What are you kicking me like that for, Bob?"

And then mother laughed a little and said, "Very well, then. Only don't walk on the line or near the tunnel or near corners."

It was the very next day that mother had to stay in bed because her head ached and her hands burned hot. She could not eat anything, and had a sore throat.

In the evening, Peter was sent to fetch the doctor. The doctor's name was W. W. Forrest and he came at once. He talked to Peter on the way back. He seemed a most charming man. When he had seen mother, he said it was just influenza and that she would be fine soon.

"I suppose you'll want to be head-nurse," he said to Bobbie, who was greatly relieved to hear that mother would be fine soon.

"Well, then, I'll have some medicine sent down. Keep up a good fire and give her some beef tea once the fever goes down."

He wrote down the list, but when Bobbie showed it to her mother, she laughed.

"Nonsense," mother said, lying in bed, "I can't afford all that rubbish."

When Roberta went downstairs after giving her mother a good sponging, she told Phil and Peter what the doctor had said, and the mother's response.

"And now," she said, "there's no one but us to do anything, and we've got to do it."

Mrs. Viney was sent to the village to get as much brandy, soda water and beef tea as she could buy for a shilling.

"We must find out some way to get all the things the doctor had said. Now both of you think as hard as you can," Bobbie said, frowning.

They did think.

Later on, when Bobbie had gone up to sit with mother, the other two got busy with scissors, white sheet, a paintbrush, and a pot of black ink. They messed up the first sheet, so they took another out of the linen cupboard.

Bobbie's bed had been moved into mother's room, and she got up to fix the fire several times in the night, and to give her mother milk and soda water. Mother kept muttering to herself in her sleep. Early next morning Bobbie heard her name, and jumping out of bed, she ran to her mother's bedside.

"Oh–ah, yes–I think I was asleep," mother said. "My poor little dear, I do hate to give you all this trouble. I shall be all right in a day or two."

"Yes," Bobbie said and tried to smile.

Her eyes were sore with lack of sleep, but she tidied the room and arranged everything neatly before the doctor came. It was around half past eight when the doctor knocked at the door.

"Everything going on all right, 'little nurse?'" he asked. "Did you get the brandy?"

"I've got the brandy," Bobbie said, "in a little flat bottle."

"I didn't see the grapes or the beef tea, though," he said.

"No," Bobbie said, firmly, "but you will tomorrow."

"Now you get Mrs. Viney to sit with your mother, you eat a good breakfast and go straight to bed and sleep till dinner-time. We can't afford to have the 'head-nurse' ill," said the nice doctor.

That morning when the 9.15 came out of the tunnel, the old gentleman in the first-class carriage put down his newspaper, and got ready to wave his hand to the three children on the fence. But today there was only one. And that was Peter. He was pointing at a large white sheet nailed against the fence. On the sheet there were thick black letters more than a foot long. The words were quite easy to read—LOOK OUT AT THE STATION.

The old gentleman looked out, and at first he saw nothing unusual. It was only just as the train was beginning to puff and start again that he saw Phyllis. She was quite out of breath with running.

"Oh," she said, "I thought I'd missed you. My

bootlaces would keep coming out and I fell over them twice. Here, take it."

She thrust a warm, dampish letter into his hand as the train moved. He leaned back in his corner and opened it. The letter read—

"Dear Mr. 'We-do-not-know-your-name,'

Mother is ill and the doctor says to give her the things mentioned at the end of the letter, but she says she can't afford it. We do not know anybody here but you. Father is away and we do not know the address. He will pay you, or if he has lost all his money, or anything, Peter will pay you when he is a man. We promise it on our honor. We do not know what train you come down by, so would you please give the parcel to the stationmaster? Say it is for Peter who was sorry about the coals. He will know.

Roberta.

Phyllis.

Peter."

Then came the list of things the doctor had

ordered. The old gentleman read it through once, and his eyebrows went up. He had read it thrice before putting it in his pocket. He then continued reading 'The Times.'

At about six that evening, there was a knock at the backdoor. The three children rushed to open it, and there stood the friendly porter with a big hamper, which he dropped on the kitchen floor.

"The old gentleman asked me to fetch it up straightaway," he said.

"Thank you very much," Peter said.

"I am sorry your mother is not well. I've brought her a bit of sweetbrier."

"Thank you very much," Peter said.

The porter left after talking to the children for a while.

Impatiently the children undid the hamper. All the things they had asked for were there—plenty of them. Also a good many things they had not asked for, like peaches, port wine, two chickens, and a cardboard box of big red roses with long stalks. There was a letter, too. It read—

"Dear Roberta, Phyllis and Peter,

Here are the things you want. Your mother will want to know where they came from. Tell her a friend who heard she was unwell sent them. When she is well again you must tell her all about it, of course. And if she says you ought not to have asked for the things, tell her that I say you were quite right, and that it is my pleasure to have this opportunity.

G. P."

"I think we were right," Phyllis said.

"Right? Of course we were right," Bobbie said.

"But at the same time I don't exactly look forward to telling mother the whole truth about it," Peter said with his hands in his pockets.

CHAPTER 5

A New Friend

The children's mother recovered after about a fortnight. The children knew they should thank their friend for his kindness. So they displayed a banner with the following message—

'*She Is Nearly Well. Thank You—To The 'Green Dragon.'*

The old gentleman saw it, and waved a cheerful response from the train.

The children realized that it was time they told their mother what they had done while she was ill. And it did not seem nearly as easy as they had thought it would be. Nevertheless they did it. Mother was extremely angry. She was angrier than they had ever known her. This was horrible. But it was much worse when she suddenly began to cry. All at once everyone found themselves taking part in a crying party. Mother stopped first.

She dried her eyes and said, "I'm sorry I was so angry."

"We didn't mean to be naughty, mummy," sobbed Bobbie.

Peter and Phyllis sniffed in unison.

"Now, listen," mother said, "it's quite true that we're poor, but we have enough to live on. You mustn't go telling everyone about our affairs. It's not right. And you must never, ever ask strangers to give you things."

They all hugged her and promised that they would never do it again.

"Now I'll write a letter to your old gentleman, and thank him for his kindness."

So when mother was well enough, she wrote a letter to the old gentleman and the children took the letter down to the stationmaster. They went down to the porter's room and talked to him. He told them that his name was Perks and that he was married with three children. It was on this day that the children first learnt that all engines were not alike. The children agreed, as they went home in the evening, that the porter was indeed very nice.

The next day was Roberta's twelfth birthday. She was out in the garden, all alone. The others had asked her to keep out of the way as they prepared her birthday surprise. Now that she was alone, she had time to think. She wondered about what her mother had said when she was down with fever.

"Oh, what a doctor's bill there'll be for this!" her mother had muttered.

She walked around the garden and the more she thought of the doctor's bill, the less she liked the idea of it. Then suddenly, she made up her mind. She went out through the side door of the garden and walked along until she came to the bridge that crossed the canal and led to the village—and here she waited. Presently there came the sound of wheels. It was the doctor's dogcart.

He stopped and called out, "Hello, 'head-nurse!' Want a lift?"

"I wanted to see you," Bobbie said.

"Your mother's not worse, I hope?" asked the doctor.

"No—but—"

"Well, skip in then, and we'll go for a drive."

Bobbie climbed in and the brown horse was made to turn round.

"This is mind-blowing," Bobbie said, as the dogcart flew along the road by the canal.

"Now, then, what's the trouble?" asked the doctor.

Bobbie fidgeted with the hook of the driving apron.

"Come on, out with it," goaded the doctor.

"It's rather hard, you see," Bobbie said, "to come out with it because of what mother said."

"What *did* mother say?"

"She said I am not supposed to go telling everyone that we're poor. But you aren't everyone, *are* you?"

"Not at all," said the doctor, cheerfully.

"Well, I know doctors are very extravagant— I mean expensive. Mrs. Viney told me that *her* doctoring only cost *her* two pence a week because she belonged to a club. She told me all about it."

"Yes?"

"I thought I'd ask you—can't we too be in the club, like Mrs. Viney?"

The doctor was silent.

"You aren't cross with me, *are* you?" Bobbie asked, in a very small voice.

"Cross? How could I be? You're a very sensible little woman. Now look here, don't you worry. I'll make things all right for your mother, even if I have to make a special and brand new club just for her. Well, we must be turning back. And, remember, you aren't to worry about doctor's bills or you'll be ill yourself."

When Bobbie parted from the doctor at the top of the field that ran down from the road to Three Chimneys, she did not feel that she had done anything wrong.

Bobbie had just enough time to dress herself before a bell rang.

"There!" Phyllis said coming to her. "That's to announce that the surprise is ready."

Bobbie went into the dining room, feeling rather shy. When she opened the door, she found herself, as it seemed, in a new world of light, flowers and music. Mother, Peter and Phyllis were standing in a row at the end of the table. There were twelve candles on the table, one for each of Roberta's years.

"Dear Bob! Many happy returns of the day!" they cried out together. "Three cheers for our Bobbie!"

Bobbie felt close to tears. But before she had time to begin, they were all kissing and hugging her.

"Now," mother said, "look at your presents."

They were very nice presents. There was a green and red needle-book that Phyllis had made herself in secret moments. There was mother's beautiful little silver brooch, shaped like a buttercup. Bobbie had loved it for years. There was also a pair of blue glass vases from Mrs. Viney. And there were three birthday cards with pretty pictures and wishes.

"And now look at the table," mother said.

There was a cake on the table covered with

white sugar, with 'Dear Bobbie' written on it in pink sweets, and there were buns and jam.

"That's my present," Peter said, suddenly dumping down his much-adored steam engine on the table in front of her. It was full of sweets.

"Oh, Peter!" cried Bobbie. "Not your own dear little engine that you're so fond of?"

"Oh, no," Peter said, very promptly, "not the engine, only the sweets."

Bobbie couldn't help her face changing a little— not so much because she was disappointed at not getting the engine, but because she had thought it so very noble of Peter—and now she felt she had been silly to even think it. It now seemed greedy to have expected the engine as well as the sweets. Peter noticed her face change.

He hesitated a minute; then his face changed, too, and he said, "I mean not *all* the engine. I'll let you go halves if you like."

"You're a brick!" cried Bobbie. "It's a splendid present!"

She said no more aloud, but thought to herself, 'that was awfully nice of Peter because I know he didn't mean to. Well, the broken half shall be my half of the engine. I'll get it mended and give it back to Peter for his birthday.'

CHAPTER 6

Bobbie's Ride in the Engine

From the very next morning, Bobbie awaited an opportunity to get Peter's engine repaired secretly. The opportunity came the next afternoon when mother went by train to the nearest town for shopping. Peter and Phyllis went with her. After they left, Bobbie went down to the railway. She went along the line to the end of the platform and hid behind a bush on the other side. She crouched down with the toy engine wrapped up in brown paper under her arm. Thus she waited patiently till the next train came in and stopped. Bobbie went across and stood beside the engine. She had never been so close to an engine before. It looked much larger and harder than she had expected. The engine driver and fireman did not see her. They were leaning out on the other side.

"If you please," Roberta said, but the engine was blowing off steam and no one heard her.

It seemed to her that the only way would be to climb onto the engine and pull at their coats. The step was high, but she managed to jump in and fell on the great heap of coals. And just as she did, the engine driver, who had not noticed her, started the engine. By the time Bobbie had picked herself up, the engine had started moving. All sorts of dreadful thoughts came to her. She knew there were express trains that went on for hundreds of miles without stopping. If this was one of them, how would she get home again?

The train was going faster and faster. She tried to speak but the men had their backs towards her. Suddenly she put out her hand and caught hold of the nearest sleeve. The man turned with a start. They stood looking at each other in silence for a minute. Then they both broke the silence at the same time.

"You're a naughty little girl, that's what you are," said the fireman.

Roberta burst into tears.

Seeing her frightened, they made her sit down on an iron seat in the cab and waited till she stopped crying. They silently waited for an explanation while she dried her eyes.

"Please, Mr. Engineer," she said, "I did call out to you from the line, but you didn't hear and I just

climbed up to touch you on the arm and then I fell onto the coals. I am so sorry. Please don't be cross!"

She sniffed again.

"We aren't much *cross*," said the fireman. "It isn't that every day a little girl tumbles into our coal bunker, is it, Bill? What did you do it for?"

"That's the point," agreed Bill, the engine driver, "what *did* you do it for?"

Bobbie was still crying.

The engine driver patted her on the back and said, "Here, cheer up, mate."

"I wanted," Bobbie said, "to ask you if you'd kindly mend this."

She picked up the brown paper parcel from among the coals, unrolled the brown paper, and disclosed the toy engine. Both the driver and the fireman took the little engine and looked at it.

"My trade is driving an engine, not mending her," said Bill. "And how are we going to get you back to your friends and relations?"

"If you'll put me down at the next stop," Bobbie said, "and lend me the money for a third-class ticket, I'll reach home. I'll pay you back, I promise."

"You're a little lady, every inch," said Bill, relenting suddenly and completely. "We'll see you get home safe. And about this engine—Jim— can you use a soldering iron? I think a little bit of it will do."

"Yes, that's what father said," Bobbie explained eagerly.

As her engine was being mended, Bobbie began chatting with Jim and saw how a real engine worked. Bobbie felt that the three of them were now friends for life. At Stacklepoole Junction, they handed her over to the guard of a returning train—a friend of theirs.

She reached home in time for tea and felt as though her mind would burst with the experience of her recent adventure.

"Where have you been?" asked the others.

"To the station, of course," Bobbie said.

But she would not tell a word of her adventure till the appointed day. On the appointed day, she mysteriously led them to the station and proudly introduced them to her friends, Bill and Jim. They handed her the toy engine and it was just as good as new.

"Good-bye—oh, good-bye," Bobbie said, just before the engine screamed good-bye.

And the three children went home up the hill—Peter hugging the engine happily.

CHAPTER 7

Prisoners and Captives

One day, mother had gone to Maidbridge alone and the children were to receive her at the station on her return. Loving the station as they did, they went there almost an hour before the train was to arrive. It happened to be a very rainy day and, for July, very cold too. They decided to wait on the UP side, for the DOWN platform looked very wet indeed.

As they waited, the UP train came and went. The children watched its taillights till it disappeared round the curve of the line, and then they turned towards the General Waiting Room. There had been just a few people before, but now they saw a large crowd on the platform "Oh!" cried Peter, with a thrill of joyous excitement. "Something's happened! Come on!"

They ran down the platform. When they got to the crowd, they could see nothing but the damp backs and elbows of the people on the outer circle of the crowd. Everybody was talking at once. It was evident that something had happened.

Then they heard the voice of the stationmaster—firm and official.

"Now, then—move along there. I'll attend to this, if you please."

But the crowd did not move. And then came a voice that thrilled the children. The voice spoke in a foreign language. It was neither French nor German and not Latin either.

"Sounds like French to me," said the stationmaster.

"It isn't French!" cried Peter.

"What is it then?" asked more than one voice.

The crowd fell back a little to see who had spoken, and Peter pressed forward, so that when the crowd closed up again he was in the front rank.

"I don't know what it is," Peter said, "but it isn't French. I know that."

At last he saw the man who was at the center of the crowd. A man with long hair and wild eyes, with shabby clothes—a man whose hands and lips trembled and who spoke again as his eyes fell on Peter.

"Try him with French if you know so much about it," said a farmer from the crowd.

"*Parlay voo Frongsay?*" began Peter, boldly.

The man with the wild eyes came away from the wall he had been leaning against and sprang forward to take Peter's hands. He began to pour forth a flood of words that Peter could not understand but knew the sound of.

"There!" he said. *"That's* French."

"What does he say?"

"I don't know," Peter was obliged to admit.

"Here," said the stationmaster again, "I'll deal with this case."

As the crowd got away, Phyllis and Bobbie got near to Peter. Peter shook the man's hands warmly and looked at him as kindly as he could.

"Take him into your room," Bobbie whispered to the stationmaster. "Mother can talk French. She'll be here by the next train."

The stationmaster took the arm of the stranger; this time not unkindly. Bobbie and Phil took hold of his hand and explained in whatever little French they could manage that their mother would be here soon and that she spoke French.

Once inside the stationmaster's room Peter had an idea. He pulled an envelope out of his pocket, and showed that it was half full of foreign stamps.

"Look here," he said, "let's show him these."

They showed him an Italian stamp, and pointing at it made signs of question with their eyebrows. He shook his head. Then they showed him a Norwegian stamp—the common blue kind it was—and again he signed *no*. Then he took the envelope from Peter's hand and searched among the stamps with a trembling hand. At last he pointed to a Russian stamp.

"He's Russian!" cried Peter.

At that instant, the train from Maidbridge was signaled.

"I'll stay with him till you bring mother in," Bobbie said.

Bobbie was still holding the stranger's hand when Peter, Phyllis and the stationmaster came back with mother. The Russian rose and bowed ceremoniously. Then mother spoke in French, and he replied—haltingly at first, but then fluently.

"Well, Ma'am, what's it all about?" the stationmaster asked eagerly.

"Oh," mother said, "it's all right. He's a Russian, and he's lost his ticket. I'm afraid he's very ill. If you don't mind, I'll take him home with me now. He's really quite worn out. I'll run down and tell you all about him tomorrow. He's a great man in his own country, writes books—beautiful books— I've read some of them. I'll tell you all about it tomorrow."

She spoke again in French to the Russian, and everyone could see the surprise and pleasure and gratitude in his eyes. He got up and bowed politely to the stationmaster, and the children left with mother and the Russian.

"You girls run home and light a fire in the sitting room," mother said, "and Peter run and get the doctor."

But it was Bobbie who went for the doctor.

"I hate to tell you," she said breathlessly when she came upon him, "but mother's got a very shabby Russian. We found him at the station and I believe he too won't have money to pay the bills."

And then she told him whatever she could. When Bobbie and the doctor reached the Three Chimneys, the Russian was sitting in the armchair in front of a nice fire, sipping tea.

"The man seems worn out in mind and body," the doctor said. "The cough's bad, but it's nothing that cannot be cured. He ought to go straight to bed, and let him have a fire at night."

Mother made her bed for him and gave him father's clothes. When Bobbie came in with more wood for the fire, she noticed the mark on the nightshirt, and looked over at the open trunk lying on the floor. All the things she could see were father's. Then father hadn't taken his clothes with him!

Bobbie slipped from the room, her heart beating like a hammer. Why hadn't father taken his clothes? She did not know what to make of it.

When mother came out of the room, Bobbie flung herself at her, tightly clasping her arms around mother's waist, and whispered,

"Mother—Daddy isn't—isn't *dead, is* he?"

"My darling, no! What made you think of anything so horrible?"

"I—I don't know," Bobbie said.

Mother gave her a hurried hug.

"Daddy was *quite*, quite well when I heard from him last," she said, "and he'll come back to us some day."

Later on, when the Russian stranger had been made comfortable for the night, mother came into the girls' room. She was to sleep there in Phyllis' bed, and Phyllis was to have a mattress on the floor—a most amusing adventure for Phyllis.

As mother came in, two white figures started up, and two eager voices called, "Now, mother, tell us all about the Russian gentleman."

A white shape hopped into the room. It was Peter, dragging his quilt behind him like the tail of a white peacock.

"I'm very tired," mother said.

Bobbie knew by her voice that mother had been crying, but the others didn't know.

"Well, it's a story long enough to make a whole book. He's a writer and has written beautiful books. In Russia, at the time of the Czar, no one dared to say anything about the rich people doing wrong. If one did, he one was sent to prison."

"But they can't," Peter said. "People go to prison only when they've done something wrong."

"Yes, that's so in England, but in Russia things are different. I've read the book for which he was sent to prison. For three years he was kept in a damp and dreadful dungeon, with hardly any light. In prison, all alone for three years!"

Mother's voice trembled a little and stopped suddenly.

"Well, then they took him out and sent him to Siberia—a convict chained to other convicts—wicked men who'd done all sorts of crimes. Oh, it's all too terrible! And at last he got to the mines, and he was condemned to stay there for life—for life, just for writing a good, noble, splendid book."

"How did he get away?"

"When the war started, some of the Russian prisoners were allowed to volunteer as soldiers. And he volunteered. But he deserted at the first chance he got, and while he was in the mines, some friends managed to get a message to him that his wife and children had escaped and come to England. So then he came here to look for them."

"Had he got their address?" asked Peter.

"No, just England. He was going to London, and he thought he had to change at our station, and then he found he'd lost his ticket, as well as his purse."

"Oh, do you think he'll find them? I mean his wife and children."

"I hope so. Oh, I hope and pray that he'll find his wife and children again."

Even Phyllis now perceived that mother's voice was very unsteady.

"Why, mother," she said, "you look very sorry!"

Mother didn't answer for a minute.

Then she said, "Dears, when you say your prayers ask God to show His mercy on all prisoners and captives."

"To show His mercy," Bobbie repeated slowly, "upon *all* prisoners and captives. Is that right, mother?"

"Yes," mother said, "upon all prisoners and captives. *All prisoners and captives.*"

CHAPTER 8

The Cherries and the Saviors

The Russian gentleman recovered fast and on the third day he was well enough to come into the garden. A basket chair was put out for him and he sat there, dressed in father's clothes that were too big for him. He no longer appeared tired and frightened. He smiled at the children whenever he saw them. They, too, tried their best to make him feel happy.

Mother wrote several letters to people she thought might know the whereabouts of the Russian gentleman's wife and family. She wrote to the Members of Parliament and Editors of papers, and Secretaries of Societies.

One day, Phyllis had an idea. She asked the others, "Do you remember Perks (the porter) promising me the very first strawberries out of his own garden? Well, I think they're ripe now. Let's go down and see."

Peter and Bobbie agreed that it was going to be a good surprise and so they went to the station. They had not been there for the last few days.

They found Perks busy reading his newspaper. He greeted them coldly and went on reading the paper. There was a long, uncomfortable silence, which was finally broken after a lot of coaxing from the children. He was cross with the children as he felt they had neglected to tell him the story of the Russian.

However, once he had heard the whole story, he came back to his old cheerful self and asked them to come over with him to check the strawberries.

"If there are any ripe ones, and you do give them to me," Phyllis said, "you won't mind if I give them to the poor Russian, *will* you?"

Perks narrowed his eyes and then raised his eyebrows.

"So it was the strawberries you came down for this afternoon, eh?" he said.

This was an awkward moment for Phyllis. To say yes would seem rude and greedy, and unkind to Perks. But she knew if she said *no*, she would not be pleased with herself afterwards.

"Yes," she said, "it was."

But then once again, Perks excused his young friends.

The Russian gentleman was so delighted with the strawberries, that the three racked their brains to find some other surprise for him. But all the racking did not bring out any idea more novel than wild cherries. And this idea occurred to them next morning. They knew the cherry trees grew along the rocky face of the cliff, out of which the mouth of the tunnel opened. It was not far from Three Chimneys.

Near the tunnel was a flight of steps leading down to the line; just a series of wooden bars—very steep and narrow—more like a ladder than a stair.

"We'd better get down," Peter said, "I'm sure the cherries would be quite easy to get from the side of the steps."

So they went towards the little swing gate at the top of these steps.

And they were almost at the gate when Bobbie said, "Hush. Stop! What's that?"

That was a very odd noise indeed—a soft rustling noise.

"Look," cried Peter, "the tree over there!"

The tree he pointed to was one of those that have rough gray leaves and white flowers. It was moving like a live creature; walking down the side of the cutting.

"It's moving!" cried Bobbie. "Oh, look! And so are the others! It's like the woods in 'Macbeth'."

"It's magic!" Phyllis said, breathlessly. "I always knew this railway was enchanted."

It really did seem a little like magic, as all the trees, for about twenty yards of the opposite bank, seemed to be slowly walking down towards the railway line. The children watched breathlessly. Some stones and loose earth fell down and rattled on the railway metals far below.

"It's *all* coming down," Peter tried to say, but his voice came out in a squeak.

Suddenly, rock and trees, grass and bushes came down with a rushing sound. The entire cliff side slipped right away and fell on the line with a huge crash. A cloud of dust rose up.

"Oh!" Peter said, awestruck.

"Look what a great mound it's made!" exclaimed Bobbie.

"Ye-e-s," Peter said, slowly.

"Ye-s-s-s-s-s-s," he said again, still more slowly. Then he almost screamed, "The 11.29 down hasn't gone by yet. We must let them know at the station, or there'll be a most frightful accident!"

"Let's run," said Bobbie and began to run towards the station.

But Peter cried, "Come back! We do not have so much time."

"If we only had something red," Peter said thoughtfully, "we could go round the corner and wave to the train."

"We might wave, anyway."

"They'd only think it was just *us*, as usual. We've waved so often before. Anyway, let's get down."

They got down the steep stairs. Phyllis was red-faced and damp with anxiety.

"Oh, how hot I am!" she said. "I wish we hadn't put on our - - -" she stopped short, and then ended in quite a different tone—"our flannel petticoats!!"

Bobbie turned at the bottom of the stairs.

"Oh, yes!" she cried. *"They're* red! Let's take them off."

So, Bobbie and Phyllis took of their petticoats and ran along the railway. They reached the corner that hid the mound from the straight line of railway. They made six flags out of the petticoats. Peter looked at the watch again. He took out his small knife and cut the branches of two small plants to make a flagstaff. Two of the flags were set up in heaps of loose stones between the sleepers of the down line. Then Phyllis and Roberta each took a flag, and stood ready to wave it as soon as the train came in sight.

"I shall have the other two myself," Peter said, "because it was my idea to wave something red."

And so the three waited with the flags in their hands, by the railway line. They waited for a very long time. Phyllis grew impatient.

"I suppose the watch is wrong, and the train's gone by," she said.

Bobbie too began to feel sick with suspense. Her hands grew very cold and trembled at the thought of what might happen if the train did not stop and crashed into the mound. Just then they heard the distant rumble and hum of the metals, and a puff of white steam showed far away along the stretch of line.

"Stand firm," Peter said, "and wave like mad! Don't stand on the line, Bobbie!"

The train came rattling along fast, very fast.

"They can't see us! They won't see us! It's all no good!" cried Bobbie.

The two little flags on the line swayed as the nearing train shook, and loosened the heaps of loose stones that held them up. It seemed that the train came on as fast as ever. It was very near now.

"Stand back!" cried Peter, suddenly, and he dragged Phyllis back by the arm.

But Bobbie cried, "Not yet, not yet!" and waved her two flags right over the line.

The engine looked black and enormous.

"Oh, stop! Stop! Stop!" cried Bobbie.

No one heard her. The engine slackened swiftly and stopped, not twenty yards from the place where Bobbie's two flags waved over the line. She saw the great black engine stop dead, but somehow she could not stop waving the flags. Peter and Phyllis ran to the engine driver who had by now jumped out, and told him what had happened. When they turned back they saw Bobbie lying across the line. Her hands were still gripped to the sticks of the little, red, flannel flags. The engine driver picked her up, carried her to the train, and laid her on the cushions of a first-class carriage.

"She has fainted," he said, "poor little woman."

They sat by Bobbie on the blue cushions, and the train ran back. Before it reached their station, Bobbie had sighed and opened her eyes. This cheered the others wonderfully.

When they reached the station, the three were the heroes of the day. The praises they got for their 'prompt action,' 'common sense,' and 'ingenuity' were enough to have turned anybody's head. Phyllis enjoyed herself thoroughly. She had never been a real heroine before, and the feeling was great. Peter's ears got very red, yet he too enjoyed himself.

"You'll hear from the company about this, I expect," said the stationmaster.

The children happily went back to the Three Chimneys.

CHAPTER 9

Valor and Two Rewards

All the editors and secretaries of the various societies and members of parliament had answered mother's letters very politely, but none of them could tell where the wife and children of the Russian were. Bobbie racked her brains to think of some way of helping the Russian gentleman to find them, but could not think of anything.

One morning, not long after the landslide, a letter came. It was addressed to Peter, Bobbie and Phyllis. They opened it with great enthusiasm. The letter said—

"Dear Sir, and Ladies,

We wish to make a small presentation to you, for your courageous and prompt action that averted a terrible accident. The presentation will take place at the station at three o'clock, on the 30th of this month if this time and place is convenient to you.

Yours faithfully,

Jabez Inglewood,

Secretary, Great Northern and Southern Railway Co."

There never had been a prouder moment in the lives of the three children. They rushed to mother with the letter, and she was overwhelmed.

"But if the presentation is money, you must say, 'Thank you, but we'd rather not take it,'" mother said.

They wrote a reply to their invitation and each made a copy and signed it separately. The threefold letter ran—

"Dear Mr. Jabez Inglewood,

Thank you very much. We had not thought of reward, as we had done it to save the train. We are glad to have received your letter and thank you very much. The time and place you mentioned is quite convenient to us. Thanking you once more.

Your affectionate little friend,"

Then came the name.

When at last—after what seemed like ages—the great day arrived, the three children went down to the station at the proper time. Everything that happened seemed like a dream. The stationmaster came out to meet them and led them into the waiting room. The room looked quite different. A carpet had been spread out and it was beautifully decorated with flowers. Quite a number of people were there besides the porter. They recognized several people who had been in the train on *the red-flannel-petticoat day*. Best of all, their own old gentleman was there, and he came forward to shake hands with them. Everybody sat down, and the District Superintendent gave quite a long speech. It made the children blush and get hot about the ears. He said all sorts of nice things about their bravery and presence of mind, and when he finished, everyone applauded. After him, the old gentleman got up and said things too. And then he called the children one by one and gave each of them a beautiful gold watch and chain. And inside each watch was engraved the name of the watch's new owner—

"From the Directors of the Northern and Southern Railway, in grateful recognition of the courageous and prompt action which averted an accident in 1905."

After this, Peter made a speech and thanked

them for their kind gesture. The people stood up applauding, as the children walked away–slowly at first, but soon racing up the hill to Three Chimneys with their watches held tight in their hands.

"I did want to talk to the old gentleman about something else," Bobbie said almost out of breath once they reached home.

"What did you want to say?" asked Phyllis.

"I'll tell you when I've thought about it more," Bobbie said.

So when she had thought a little more, she wrote a letter. It read–

"My dearest old gentleman,

I want most awfully to ask you something. If you could get out of the train and go by the next, I would be happy. I do not want you to give me *anything;* I only want to talk to you about a prisoner and a captive.

Your loving little friend,

Bobbie."

She asked the stationmaster to give the letter

to the old gentleman. The next day, she asked Peter and Phyllis to come down to the station with her. She explained her idea to them and they approved thoroughly. They reached the station just in time to find the gentleman coming forward to meet them.

"Hello," he said, shaking hands with them all in turn. "This is a very great pleasure."

"It was good of you to get out," Bobbie said politely.

He took her arm and drew her into the waiting room. Phyllis and Peter followed.

"Well?" the old gentleman said. "What is it?"

"Oh, please!" Bobbie said.

"Yes?" the old gentleman said.

"What I mean to say—" Bobbie said.

"Say it," he said.

"Well, then," Bobbie said—and out came the story of the Russian, who had written the beautiful book and had been sent to prison and to Siberia for just that.

"And what we want more than anything in the world is to find his wife and children for him," she continued, "but we don't know how. But you must be very clever, or you wouldn't be a Director of the Railway."

"Hum," the old gentleman said, "what did you say the name was–Fryingpansky?"

"No, no," Bobbie said earnestly. "I'll write it down for you."

She wrote down 'Szezepansky' on a nice little notebook that the old gentleman gave, and said, "That's how you write it. You call it Shepansky."

The old gentleman read the name and exclaimed "That man! Bless my soul! Why, I've read his book! It's translated into every European language. It is a fine book. And so your mother took him in like the 'Good Samaritan'. Well, well. I'll tell you something, your mother must be a very good woman."

"Of course, she is!" Phyllis said, in astonishment.

"And you're a very good man," Bobbie said, very shyly.

"You flatter me," the old gentleman said, with a smile. "Well then, I'll only say that I'm very glad you came to me about this—very glad, indeed. And I shouldn't be surprised if I found out something very soon. I know a great many Russians in London, and every Russian knows 'his' name. Now tell me all about yourselves."

But the children did not come up with anything.

"All right, we'll have an examination," the old gentleman said. "You all sit on the table, and I'll sit on the bench and ask questions."

He did, and out came their names and ages: their father's name and business: how long they had lived at Three Chimneys and a great deal more. Very soon, the next train came chugging in and it was time for him to leave.

About ten days after the interview in the

waiting room, the three children were sitting on the top of the biggest rock in the field, below their house, watching the 5.15 steam away from the station along the bottom of the valley. They saw one person who got out at the station, left the road and opened the gate that led across the fields to Three Chimneys.

"Who on earth!" Peter cried, scrambling down.

"Let's go and see," Phyllis said.

So they went. And when they got near enough, they saw it was their old gentleman himself.

"Hello!" shouted the children, waving their hands.

"Hello!" replied the old gentleman, waving his hat. Then the three started to run and when they got to him they hardly had breath left to say— "How do you do?"

"Good news," he said. "I've found your Russian friend's wife and child."

"Here," he said to Bobbie, "you run on

and tell him. The other two will show me the way."

Bobbie ran. As soon as she told it to mother, mother told it to the Russian. The Russian sprang up with a cry that made Bobbie's heart leap and then tremble—a cry of love and longing she had never heard before. He took mother's hand and kissed it gently and reverently, and then sinking down in his chair, he covered his face with his hands and sobbed.

Finally, Peter ran down to the village for buns and cakes. The girls got tea ready and together they all had a delightful time.

Then mother turned to the old gentleman and thanked him for all his help. He bowed to her and left the Russian, the children and their mother amidst rejoicing and celebrations.

Being rewarded with watches had been great, but helping to bring a family together seemed to be a greater reward.

CHAPTER 10

A Birthday Celebration

"That's a beautiful little brooch you've got on, miss," Perks said. "I have never seen anything look so real. It appears to be a real buttercup."

"Yes," Bobbie said, glad and flushed by this approval.

"I never thought it would be mine, my very own. Then mother gave it to me for my birthday."

"Oh, did you have a birthday?" Perks asked, quite surprised.

"Yes," Bobbie said. "When's your birthday, Mr. Perks?"

The children were taking tea with Mr. Perks in the porter's room.

"My birthday?" Perks asked, quite surprised. "I gave up celebrating my birthday long before you were even born."

"But you must have been born sometime, you know," Phyllis said, thoughtfully.

"If you really want to know, it was thirty-two years ago, on the fifteenth of this month."

"Then why don't you keep it?" asked Phyllis.

"I've got something else to take care of, besides birthdays," Perks said, briefly.

"Oh! What?" Phyllis asked.

"The kids and the Missus," said Perks.

The children walked back home, each of them lost in their thoughts and thinking hard what they could do for him on his birthday.

"It seems horrid that nobody celebrates his birthday," Bobbie said.

The next morning, during breakfast, mother said, "I've sold another story, so there'll be buns for tea."

Peter, Phyllis, and Bobbie exchanged glances with each other, six glances in all.

Then Bobbie said, "Mother, would you mind if we didn't have the buns for tea today, but on the fifteenth? That's next Thursday."

"I don't mind when you have them, dear," mother said. "But why?"

"Because it's Perks' birthday," Bobbie said. "He's thirty-two and he says he doesn't celebrate his birthday any more, because he's got to take care of the kids and the missus."

"You mean his wife and children?" mother asked.

"Yes," Phyllis replied.

"We thought we'd make a nice birthday for him," Peter said.

"And we agreed that next bun-day we'd ask you if we could."

"I see. Certainly," mother said.

And then they all agreed upon having Perks other name—Albert—on the cake.

They considered the gifts they could give Perks on his birthday.

"There must be lots of people in the village who'd like to celebrate his birthday. Let's go round and ask everybody," Peter said.

"Mother said we weren't to ask people for things," Bobbie said, doubtfully.

"For us, she meant, silly, not for other people. I'll ask the old gentleman too. You see if I don't," Peter said.

They began with the old lady at the post office,

but she said she didn't see why Perks should have a birthday when many others did not.

"No," Bobbie said, "I would like everyone to have one. Only we know when his is."

"Mine's tomorrow," said the old lady, "and much notice anyone will take of it. Now get along."

So they went.

Peter wrote down the lists of the things other people gave, in the little pocket book where he kept the numbers of his engines.

Early next morning, Bobbie and Phyllis woke quietly and cut a big bunch of roses. They put it in a basket with the needle-book that Phyllis had made for Bobbie on her birthday, and a very pretty blue necktie of Phyllis'. Then they wrote on a paper, 'For Mrs. Ransome, with love on her birthday.' Placing the paper in the basket, they carried it to the post office. They placed it on the counter there, and ran away before the old woman at the post office came into her shop.

Peter did not know of this secret adventure, but the girls told him when it turned out all right.

That morning, Peter told mother of their plans for Perks' birthday.

"There's no harm in it," mother said, "but it depends how you do it. I only hope he won't be offended and think of it as charity."

"Oh, we are doing it because we're fond of him," Phyllis said.

On the fifteenth, the children collected the gifts and went to Perks' place in the evening. His wife greeted them and they all waited for him to come home. Though Perks was very upset at first and thought it was charity, he understood when the children explained everything. He was in fact quite moved by the love and affection of his neighbors.

"I don't know if ever I was happier," he said.

Peter, Phyllis and Bobbie thought they, too, had never been happier.

CHAPTER 11

The Terrible Secret

When they first went to live at the Three
Chimneys, the children had talked a great
deal about their father. But as time passed by,
they began to speak less of him. One day, when
mother was working, Bobbie carried up her tea

to the big room, which they called 'mother's workshop.'

"Here's your tea, mother," Bobbie said.

Mother laid down her pen among the pages that were scattered all over the table, and looked at her and asked, "Bobbie, do you think Peter and Phil are forgetting father?"

"No," Bobbie said, indignantly. "Why?"

"None of you ever speak of him now," mother replied.

Bobbie stood first on one leg and then on the other.

"We often talk about him amongst ourselves," she said.

"But not to me," mother said, "Why?"

Bobbie did not find it easy to answer *why*.

"I—you—"she said and stopped. She went over to the window and looked out.

"Bobbie, come here," said her mother, and Bobbie came.

"Now," mother said, putting her arm round Bobbie, "try to tell me, dear."

Bobbie fidgeted.

"Well then," Bobbie said, "I thought you were so unhappy about daddy not being here, it made you worse when I talked about him. So I stopped doing it. And I expect Phil and Peter feel the same about it as me."

"The trouble won't last always?" Bobbie asked, in a very soft voice.

"No," mother said, "the worst will be over when father comes home to us."

"I wish I could make things easier for you," Bobbie said.

"Oh, my dear, do you think I haven't noticed how good you've all been, not quarreling nearly as much as you used to and all the little kind things you do for me?"

"Now I must get on with my work; but Bobbie," she said giving her one last squeeze, "don't say anything to the others as yet."

That evening, in the hour before bedtime, instead of reading to the children, mother told them stories of the games she and father used to play when they were children. Those were very funny stories, and the children laughed as they listened.

** ** ** ** ** ** ** ** **

After they had come to the Three Chimneys, mother had allowed them to have a piece of their own garden and they were free to plant whatever they liked there. Phyllis had planted mignonette, nasturtium and Virginia Stock in hers. Peter sowed vegetable seeds in his—carrots, onions and turnips. Bobbie planted rosebushes in her garden, but all the little new leaves of the rosebushes shriveled and withered, perhaps because she moved them from the other part of the garden in May, which is not at all the right time of the year for moving roses.

It was the day after mother had praised Bobbie and the others about not quarreling. Bobbie was digging up her dead rose plants while Peter had decided to flatten out all his forts and earthworks, with a view to making a model of the railway-tunnel, bridges, and all. Bobbie went to dump the dead red roses in one corner of the garden. When Bobbie came back from her last thorny journey with the dead rosebushes, Peter had got the rake and was using it busily.

"I was using the rake," Bobbie said.

"Well, I'm using it now!" Peter said.

"But I had it first," Bobbie said holding on to its handle.

"Then it's my turn now," Peter said.

And that was how the quarrel began.

"Don't—I said, this morning I meant to have it, didn't I, Phil?"

Phyllis said she didn't want to be mixed up in their rows.

"I wish I'd had a brother instead of two whiny little kiddy sisters," Peter said.

"I can't think why little boys were ever

invented," shouted Bobbie, and just as she said it, she looked up and saw the three long windows of mother's workshop flashing in the red rays of the sun. The sight brought back those words of praise—*'You don't quarrel like you used to do.'*

"Oh!" cried Bobbie, just as if she had been hit.

"What's the matter?" Phyllis asked.

"Take the horrid rake, then," Bobbie said to Peter.

Saying so, she suddenly let go her hold on the handle. Peter, who had been holding on to it firmly, staggered and fell over backward, the teeth of the rake between his feet.

"Serves you right," Bobbie said, before she could stop herself.

Peter lay still for half a moment—long enough to frighten Bobbie a little. Then she got really frightened, for he sat up—screamed and turned rather pale. He then lay back and began to moan, faintly but steadily. Mother put her head out of

the window, and it wasn't half a minute after which she was in the garden kneeling by the side of Peter.

"What happened, Bobbie?" mother asked.

"It was the rake," Phyllis said.

"Peter was pulling at it, so was Bobbie, and she let go and he went over."

"Stop screaming, Peter," mother said. "Come. Stop at once."

Peter stopped.

"Now," mother asked, "are you hurt?"

"If he was really hurt, he wouldn't make such a fuss," Bobbie said, still trembling with fury. "He's not a coward!"

"I think my foot's broken off, that's all," Peter said huffily and sat up.

Then he turned quite white. Mother put her arm round him.

"He is hurt," she said, "he's fainted. Here, Bobbie, sit down and take his head on your lap."

Then mother undid Peter's boots. As she took the right one off, something dripped from his foot onto the ground. It was red blood! And when the stocking came off, there were three red wounds in Peter's foot and ankle, where the teeth of the rake had bitten him.

"Run and bring some water—a basinful," mother said.

Phyllis ran and got it. Peter did not open his eyes again, till mother had tied her handkerchief round his foot. Then she and Bobbie carried him in and laid him on the brown wooden settee in the dining room. Phyllis then ran to the doctor. Mother sat by Peter, while Bobbie went out to get the tea ready.

'It's all I can do,' Bobbie thought to herself.

The doctor came and looked at the foot. He bandaged it firmly and said, "Now, do not put it down for at least a week."

"He won't be lame, or have to wear crutches or have a lump on his foot, will he?" whispered

Bobbie breathlessly to the doctor, as he was leaving.

"My aunt! No!" said Dr. Forrest. "He'll be as good as new in a fortnight."

It was when mother had gone to the gate with the doctor to take his last instructions, and Phyllis was filling the kettle for tea, that Peter and Bobbie found themselves alone.

"He says you won't be lame or anything," Bobbie said, quietly.

"Oh, course I won't be, silly," Peter said, very much relieved all the same.

"Oh, Peter, I am so sorry," Bobbie said, after a pause.

"That's all right," Peter said, gruffly.

"It was *all* my fault," Bobbie said.

"If we hadn't quarreled, it wouldn't have happened. I knew it was wrong to quarrel. I wanted to say so, but somehow I couldn't."

And so both of them patched up.

Peter was tired for many days after that, and

the settee seemed hard and uncomfortable in spite of all the pillows and soft rugs. It was terrible not to be able to go out. They moved the settee to the window. From there Peter could see the smoke of the trains winding along the valley, but he could not see the trains.

Peter had many visitors. Mrs. Perks came up to ask how he was, and so did the stationmaster and several of the village people. But still Peter felt bored.

"I do wish there was something to read," Peter said. "I've read all our books fifty times over."

"I'll go to the doctor's," Phyllis said brightly, "he's sure to have some."

"Only about how to be ill, and about people's nasty insides, I expect," Peter said.

"Perks has a whole heap of magazines which he gets from the train passengers," Bobbie said. "I'll run down and ask him."

When Bobbie reached Perks' house, she found him busy cleaning lamps.

"And how's the young gentleman?" he asked.

"Better, thanks," Bobbie said, "but he's most frightfully bored. I came to ask if you'd got any magazines you could lend him."

Perks said that he had given them to someone else, but yes, he did have a lot of illustrated papers.

"I am sure Peter would love them. I'll just wrap them with a bit of paper," said Perks.

Pulling out an old newspaper from the pile, he made a neat parcel of it.

"You're a dear," Bobbie said.

She took the parcel, and started back for home.

The papers were heavy, and while she waited at the level crossing for a train to pass by, she kept the parcel on the top of the gate. Idly, she looked at the printing on the paper that the parcel was wrapped in. Suddenly, she clutched the parcel tighter and bent her head over it. *It seemed like some horrible dream.* She began to read, but the bottom of the column was torn off—she could read no further.

She never remembered how she got home. But she went on tiptoe to her room and locked the door. Then she undid the parcel and read that printed column again, sitting on the edge of her bed, her hands and feet icy cold and her face burning. When she had read all there was, she drew a long, uneven breath.

"So now I know," she said.

What she had read was headed—

'End of the Trial. Verdict—Sentence!'

The person on trial was her *father!* The verdict was 'Guilty,' and the sentence was 'FIVE YEARS' PENAL SERVITUDE.'

"Oh, daddy," she whispered, crushing the paper hard, "it's not true. I don't believe it. You never did it! Never, never, never!"

Someone was hammering on the door.

"What is it?" Bobbie asked.

"It's me," Phyllis' voice came. "Tea's ready, and a boy's brought Peter a guinea pig. Come along down."

Bobbie thought it best to keep quiet about it for now, and she went down.

CHAPTER 12

The Hound in the Red Jersey

Bobbie knew the secret now. A sheet of old newspaper wrapped round a parcel had revealed the secret to her. And when she went down to tea, everyone noticed her red swollen eyes.

"My darling!" cried mother, "What is the matter? Has anything gone wrong?"

"I have a headache," Bobbie said. "I'm all right, really."

Tea was not a cheerful meal. Peter was so distressed by the obvious fact that something unpleasant had happened to Bobbie, that he limited his speech to repeating, 'More bread and butter, please,' at unexpectedly short intervals.

After what seemed like ages, Bobbie managed to get mother alone in her room. She locked the door and stood quietly. All through tea she had been thinking of what to say. She had decided that 'I know all,' or 'all is known to me,' or 'the terrible secret is a secret no longer,' would be proper lines to start with. But now that she and mother were alone, Bobbie found that she could not say anything. Suddenly she ran to mother and putting her arms round her, began to cry.

"Oh, mummy, oh, mummy, oh, mummy!" was all she could say over and over again.

Mother held her very close and waited. Suddenly, Bobbie broke away from her and went to the bed. From under her mattress, she pulled out the paper, which she had hidden. Holding it out, she pointed to her father's name with a finger that shook.

"Oh, Bobbie!" mother cried. "You don't *believe* it, do you? You don't believe daddy did it!"

"No," Bobbie almost shouted.

"That's all right," mother said. "It's not true. And they've shut him up in prison, but he's done nothing wrong. He's good and noble and honorable, and he belongs to us. We have to think of that, and be proud of him, and wait."

Again Bobbie clung to her mother, and again only one word came to her, but now that word was 'daddy,' and 'Oh, daddy, oh, daddy, oh, daddy!' again and again.

"Why didn't you tell me, mummy?" she asked presently.

"Are you going to tell the others?" mother asked.

"No."

"Why?"

"Because..."

"Exactly," mother said. "So you understand why I didn't tell you. We two must help each other to be brave."

"Yes," Bobbie said. "Mother, will it make you unhappier if you tell me all about it? I want to understand."

So then, sitting cuddled up close to her mother, Bobbie heard 'all about it.' She heard how those men who had asked to see father on that night, had come to arrest him, charging him with selling state secrets to the Russians. They accused him of being a spy and a traitor. She heard about the trial, and about the evidence—letters found in father's desk at the office; letters that convinced the jury that father was guilty.

"Someone else did it," mother said, "and all the evidence was against father."

"Those letters–how did they get into his desk?"

"The person who put them there was the one who was really guilty. This man had long wanted to be in father's post. He was extremely jealous because everyone thought so highly of your father. Your father never quite trusted that man."

"Couldn't we explain all that to someone?"

"Nobody will listen," mother said, very bitterly, "nobody at all. Do you suppose I've not tried everything? No, my dearest, there's nothing to be done. All we can do, you and daddy and I, is to be brave, and patient, and," she spoke very softly, "to pray."

"Mummy, I do think you're the bravest person in the world as well as the nicest!" Bobbie said.

"We won't talk of all this any more, will we,

dear?" mother said. "We must bear it and be brave. Wash your poor little round face, and let's go out into the garden for a while."

The other two were very gentle and kind to Bobbie. They thought it best not to ask her anything just then.

A week later, Bobbie managed to get away alone. Once more, she wrote a letter to the old gentleman.

"My dear friend," she wrote. "you see what is in this paper. It is not true. Father never did it. Mother says someone put the papers in father's desk. The man who got father's position afterwards had been jealous of him all along. Father, too, suspected him. But nobody listens to a word, mother says. You are so good and clever, and you easily found the Russian gentleman's wife. If you could find out who did the treason, I'm sure they would let father out of prison.

There is only mother and me who know, and we cannot do a thing. Peter and Phil don't know anything about it. I'll pray for you twice daily as long as I live, if you'll only try to find out. Imagine how you would feel if it had been your daddy! Oh, please do help me!

     With love,

     Your affectionate little friend,

     Roberta."

She cut the account of her father's trial out of the newspaper, and put it in the envelope with her letter. Then she took it down to the station, going out the back way and round by the road, so that the others would not see her. She gave the letter to the stationmaster to give to the old gentleman next morning.

** ** ** ** ** ** ** ** **

"I say," Bobbie said, once she was back home, "there's going to be a paper chase tomorrow. Perks thinks the hare will go along by the line at first."

And next morning, mother packed their lunch and allowed them out for the day to see the paper chase. They had learnt from Perks that this was a race held annually, where one person (The hare) runs ahead with a bag full of paper bits. A group of people, (The hounds), have to track him down by the bits of paper that he keeps throwing.

"If we go to the cutting," Peter said. "We shall see the workmen clearing the debris from the railway lines, even if we miss the paper chase."

The children watched the men work—clearing the lines with picks and spades and carting away the mud in wheelbarrows. So engrossed were they in watching the men that they completely forgot about the paper chase. So much so, that they jumped when a voice behind them panted, "Let me pass, please."

It was the hare—a big-boned, loose-limbed boy, with dark hair lying flat on a very damp forehead. The children stood back. The hare ran along the line and disappeared into the mouth of the tunnel.

And now, following the track of the hare, by the little white bits of scattered paper, came the hounds. There were thirty of them. They all came down the steep hill and disappeared into the dark mouth of the tunnel. The last one, in a red jersey, seemed to be extinguished by the darkness, like a candle that is blown out.

"Do you think they'll take a long time to get through?" Peter asked the workmen.

"An hour or more," said one of the workmen, looking up from his digging. It isn't so easy running in the dark. The tunnel takes two or three turns."

"Then let's cut across the top and see them come out at the other end," Peter said, "We shall get there long before they do."

The counsel seemed good, and they went. They climbed the steep steps and at last they stood on the very top of the hill, where they had so often wished to be.

"Halt!" cried Peter, and threw himself flat on the grass.

The girls also threw themselves down besides him. It was really a most exciting place to be in.

"I know the paper chase has gone long ago," Phyllis said every two minutes as they waited, and then suddenly, Peter cried, "Look out, here he comes!"

They all leaned over the wall in time to see the hare come out from the shadow of the tunnel.

"There, now," Peter said. "What did I tell you? Now for the hounds!"

Very soon came the hounds—in groups of twos, threes, sixes and sevens. They were going slowly and seemed very tired.

"There," Bobbie said, "that's all—now what shall we do?"

"Let us go over to the woods and have lunch," Phyllis said, "We can see them for miles from up here."

"Not yet," Peter said. "That's not the last. There's the one in the red jersey yet to come."

Though they waited for a long time, the boy did not appear.

"Oh, let's have lunch," Phyllis said. "I've got a pain in my stomach from being so hungry. You must have missed him when he came out with the others."

But Bobbie and Peter agreed that he had not come out with the others.

"Let's get down to the mouth of the tunnel," Peter said, "then perhaps we shall see him coming along from the inside."

And still there was no sign of the hound with the red jersey.

"Oh, do, *do* let's have something to eat," wailed Phyllis. "I shall die of hunger, and then you'll be sorry."

"Give her the sandwiches, for goodness' sake," Peter said. "Look here," he added turning to Bobbie, "perhaps we'd better have one each, too. We may need all our strength. Not more than one, though. There's no time. I think that

the red-jersey hound may have had an accident—
that's what it is."

A tunnel seems quite exciting when you see
it from inside a train. It looks very different when
you walk into it. Then you see slimy, oozy trickles
of water running down the walls and the bricks
look dull, sticky, sickly green.

It was not yet quite dark in the tunnel when
Phyllis caught at Bobbie's skirt and said, "I want
to go back. I don't like it. It'll be pitch dark in a
minute. I won't go on in the dark. I don't care
what you say, I won't."

"Don't be a silly cuckoo," Peter said, "I've got
a candle and matches."

"Come on," he said, as he lit the candle,
"we've got to go and see."

So the three went on into the deeper darkness
of the tunnel. Peter led, holding his candle and
shouted 'Hello.' Only the walls echoed back. So
he walked faster. When the others caught him
up, he was standing still, looking at a patch of red

a few feet away. There, slumped down by the curved, pebbly down line, was the red–jersey hound. His back was against the wall, his arms hung limply by his sides, and his eyes were shut.

"He has only fainted," Peter said, relieved to see the hound alive. "What on earth are we to do?"

"Can we move him?" Bobbie asked.

"I don't know, he's a big chap."

"Suppose we bathe his forehead with water. I know we haven't any, but milk's just as wet. There's a whole bottle."

"Yes," Peter said, "and they rub people's hands, I believe."

And so Peter rubbed the hands of the hound, while Phyllis splashed milk on his forehead.

And all three kept on saying, "Oh, look up, speak to me! For my sake, speak!"

CHAPTER 13

What Bobbie brought home

It was very dark in the tunnel. The candle had burnt down, and now gave a faint light.

"Oh, do look up," Phyllis implored. "I believe he's dead."

"Come out of it," Peter said, as he shook the boy by the arm.

The boy in the red-jersey let out a sigh, opened his eyes and shut them again.

"Oh, he's not dead," Phyllis said. "I knew he wasn't," and then she began to cry loudly.

At this, the boy opened his eyes and said, "What's up? I'm all right."

"Drink this," Peter said firmly, thrusting the milk bottle into the boy's mouth.

"It is milk. Do drink it," Bobbie said gently, "it'll do you good."

So he drank. And the three stood watching him in silence.

"Let him be a minute," Peter whispered, just as Phyllis was about to ask him something.

As he felt a little better after having the milk, he tried to move, but the movement ended in a groan.

"I believe I've broken my leg," he said.

"Did you tumble down?" asked Phyllis, sniffing.

"Of course not," said the boy, indignantly.

"It was one of those wires. I tripped, and when I tried to get up again, I couldn't stand, so I sat down. But how did you three get here?"

"We saw you all go into the tunnel and then we went across the hill to see you all come out. We saw all the others come out but not you. So we are a rescue party," Peter said, with pride.

"Wow! You do have guts!" remarked the boy.

"Oh, that's nothing," Peter said, modestly. "Do you think you could walk if we helped you?"

"I can try," the boy said.

And he did, but he could not.

"Oh!" he groaned. "Let me sit down. I feel like dying."

He lay down once again and closed his eyes. The others looked at each other by the dim light of the candle.

"What on earth!" Peter said.

"Look here," Bobbie said quickly, "you must go and get help. Go to the nearest house."

"Yes, that's the only thing," Peter said. "Come on."

The three of them managed to carry the boy to a safer place before he fainted again.

"Now," Bobbie said, "I'll stay with him, while you go with the longer bit of candle. Please be quick, for this bit won't burn long."

"I don't think mother would like me leaving you," Peter said, doubtfully. "Let me stay, while you and Phil go fetch help."

"No, no," Bobbie said. "You and Phil go and lend me your knife. I'll try to get his boot off before he wakes up again. Now you both hurry up."

So they hurried off. Bobbie watched their dark figures and their diminishing little light with an odd feeling of having come to the end of everything. She thought she knew now what nuns, who were bricked up alive in convent walls, felt like. Suddenly she gave herself a little shake.

'Don't be a silly little girl,' she scolded herself.

She fixed the candle bit on a broken brick

near the red-jerseyed boy's feet. Then she opened Peter's knife. It was always hard to manage—a halfpenny was generally needed to yank it open. This time, somehow, Bobbie managed to open it with her thumbnail. She broke the nail, and it hurt horribly. Then she cut the boy's bootlace, and got the boot off. She tried to pull off his stocking, but his leg was dreadfully swollen, and it did not seem to be in the proper shape. So she cut the stocking down—very slowly and carefully.

When Bobbie had got the stocking off and saw the poor leg, she felt as though the tunnel was growing darker, and the ground felt unsteady, and nothing seemed quite real.

"Silly little girl!" Roberta reprimanded Bobbie, and felt better.

She took off her white flannel petticoat and placed it under his foot as a cushion.

'Oh, what useful things flannel petticoats are!' she thought.

She hastily wet her handkerchief with milk and spread it over the swollen leg.

"Ouch! That hurts!" cried the boy, who had regained consciousness.

"Oh no, it doesn't; it's cool, really."

"What's your name?" Bobbie asked.

"Jim."

"Mine's Bobbie."

"I say, Bobbie," Jim paused, looking around.

"Yes?"

"Weren't there some more of you just now?"

"Yes, Peter and Phil—that's my brother and sister. They've gone to get someone to carry you out."

"Why didn't you go with the others?"

"Somebody had to stay with you," Bobbie said.

"Tell you what, Bobbie," said Jim, "you're a brick!"

He held out his arm and Bobbie squeezed his hand.

"I won't shake it," she explained, "because it would shake you, and that would shake your poor leg, and that would hurt. Have you got a hanky?"

"I don't expect I have."

He felt in his pocket.

"Yes, I have. What for?"

She took it and wet it with milk and put it on his forehead.

"You're a jolly good little nurse," said Jim.

She tried to talk, to amuse him and take his mind off his pain, but it was very difficult to go on talking in the dark. They had blown out the candle to save it, and presently they found themselves waiting in silence, only broken now and then by a–'You all right, Bobbie?'

** ** ** ** ** ** ** ** **

Peter and Phyllis tramped down the long way of the tunnel towards daylight, the candle–grease dripping over Peter's fingers.

"There's no end to this tunnel," Phyllis said and indeed it did seem very long.

"Stick to it," Peter said. "Everything has an end, and you get to it only if you keep on."

"Look!" he exclaimed suddenly. "There's the end of the tunnel—looks just like a pinhole in a bit of black paper, doesn't it?"

The pinhole got larger—blue lights lay along the sides of the tunnel. The children could see the gravel way that lay in front of them; the air grew warmer and sweeter. Another twenty steps and they were out in the sunshine with the green trees on both sides. Phyllis drew a long breath.

"Now, where's the nearest house, I wonder? You can't see anything here for the trees," Peter said.

"There, I can see a roof over there!" Phyllis said, pointing down the line.

"That's the signal-box," Peter said, "and you know you're not allowed to speak to the signalman on duty. It's wrong."

"I'm not afraid of doing wrong if it is to help

someone," Phyllis retorted. "Come on," she said, and started to run along the line.

So Peter ran too. It was very warm in the sunshine. Both children were hot and breathless by the time they stopped. Bending their heads back to look up at the open windows of the signal-box, they shouted 'Hi!' as loud as their breathless state allowed.

No answer!

The children climbed up the signal-box, and peeped in at the open door. The signalman was sitting on a chair tilted back against the wall. His head leaned sideways, and his mouth was open. He was fast asleep.

"My hat!" cried Peter. "Wake up!"

Peter cried in a terrible voice, for he knew that if a signalman sleeps on duty, he risks losing his job. The signalman did not move. Peter sprang to him and shook him. And slowly, yawning and stretching, the man awoke. But the moment he was awake, he leapt to his feet, put his hands to his head 'like a mad maniac,' as Phyllis said afterwards, and shouted, "Oh, my heavens, what's the time?"

"Twelve thirteen," Peter said.

And indeed it was by the white, round-faced clock on the wall of the signal-box.

The man looked at the clock, sprang to the levers, and wrenched them this way and that. An electric bell tingled, the wires and cranks creaked, and the man threw himself into a chair. He was very pale, and the sweat stood on his forehead like 'large dewdrops on a white cabbage,' as Phyllis remarked later. He was trembling and drew in large gulps of air.

Then suddenly he cried, "Thank God, you came in! Oh, thank..."

Peter quickly interrupted, "We came here to tell you something you don't know. There's a boy in the tunnel over there, and his leg is broken."

"I have not had a wink of sleep for the last five

days," said the man irritably. "What did he have to go into the tunnel for?"

"Don't you be so cross," Phyllis said, kindly. "We haven't done anything wrong except coming and waking you up to ask for help."

Then Peter explained how the boy came to be in the tunnel.

"Well," the man said, "I don't see as I can do anything. I can't leave the box."

"You might tell us where to find someone who isn't in a box, though," Phyllis said.

"There's Brigden's farm nearby. You will find someone there," he said, pointing to a house that had smoke coming out of its chimney.

"Well, goodbye then," Peter said and rushed out.

Phyllis waited back to thank the man once more, and then followed Peter across the fields to the farm.

Soon, Peter and Phyllis led some farmers, who carried with them a hurdle covered with horse-clothes to the injured boy in the tunnel. Bobbie was fast asleep and so was Jim. "Worn out with the pain," the doctor said afterwards.

"Where does he live?" the bailiff from the farm asked, when Jim had been lifted onto the hurdle.

"In Northumberland," answered Bobbie.

"I'm in school at Maidbridge," said Jim. "I suppose I've got to get back there, somehow."

"Seems to me, the doctor ought to have a look at your leg first," said the bailiff.

"Oh, bring him up to our house," Bobbie said. "It's only a little way by the road. I'm sure mother would say we ought to."

"Will your mother like you bringing home strangers with broken legs?"

"She took the poor Russian home herself," Bobbie said. "I know she'd say we ought to."

"All right," said the bailiff, "you ought to know what your mother likes."

"Are you sure your mother won't mind?" whispered Jim.

"Certain," Bobbie said.

"Then off we go with him to Three Chimneys," said the bailiff.

** ** ** ** ** ** ** ** **

Thus it happened, that mother, who was writing a story about a duchess, a scheming villain, a secret passage, and a missing will, dropped her pen as her workroom door burst open, and turned to see Bobbie hatless and red with running.

"Oh, mother," she cried, "do come down! We found a hound in a red jersey in the tunnel, and he's broken his leg and they're bringing him home."

"They ought to take him to the vet," mother said with a worried frown. "I really can't have a lame dog here."

"He's not a dog, really–he's a boy," Bobbie said, between laughing and choking.

"Then he ought to be taken home to his mother."

"His mother's dead," Bobbie said, "and his

father is in Northumberland. I told him I was sure you'd want us to bring him home. You always want to help everybody."

Mother smiled.

"Oh, well," mother said, "we must be with him."

When Jim was carried in, dreadfully white with bluish lips, mother said, "I am glad you brought him here. Now, Jim, let's get you comfortable in bed before the doctor comes!"

And Jim, looking at her kind eyes, felt a flush of new courage.

"It'll hurt rather, won't it?" he said. "I don't mean to be a coward. And I do hate to give you all this trouble."

"Don't you worry," mother said, "it's you that have the trouble—you poor dear, not us."

And she kissed him just as if he had been Peter.

CHAPTER 14

The Hound's Grandfather

Mother did not get back to her writing all that day, for Jim had to be put to bed. And when the doctor came, mother was with him all through. The children sat in the parlor downstairs, and heard the sound of the doctor's boots going backwards and forwards over the bedroom floor.

He finally came in rubbing his hands and looking pleased with himself.

"Well," he said, "that job's done. It's a nice, clean fracture, but it'll mend up all right, I've no doubt. Brave young chap."

"Now," said Dr. Forrest, "I looked in to see if one of you would come along to the surgery. There are some things that your mother will want at once, and I've given my man a day off. Would you come, Peter?"

Peter agreed happily and went with the doctor. Once they reached his house, the doctor packed up the things that mother might need for Jim's foot, and he came back home.

** ** ** ** ** ** ** ** **

"May I come in, mother?" Peter was at the door of mother's writing room.

"Yes, dear," mother said, absently, "anything wrong?"

She wrote a few more words and then laid

down her pen and began to fold up what she had written.

"I was just writing to Jim's grandfather. He lives near here, you know."

"Yes, you said so. That's what I want to say. Must you write to him, mother? Couldn't we keep Jim, and not say anything to his people till he's well? It would be such a surprise for them."

"Well, yes," mother said, laughing, "I think it would."

"You see," Peter went on, "of course the girls are all right and all that—I'm not saying anything against them. But I should like it if I had another chap to talk to sometimes."

"Yes," mother said, "I know it's dull for you, dear. But I can't help it. Next year perhaps I can send you to school—you'd like that, wouldn't you?"

"I do miss the other chaps, rather," Peter confessed, "but if Jim could stay after his leg was well, we would have a great time."

"I've no doubt you would," mother said. "Well perhaps he could stay, but you know, dear, we're not rich. I can't afford to get him everything he'll want. And he must have a nurse."

"Can't you nurse him, mother? You do nurse people so beautifully."

"That's a pretty compliment Peter, but I can't do nursing and my writing as well. That's the worst of it."

"Then you must send the letter to his grandfather?"

"Of course, he'll be very anxious."

"Well I think his grandfather can pay us for the nurse; he should be rich enough to do that. Grandfathers in books always have a lot of money."

"Well, this one isn't in a book," mother said, "and it is not right to expect something in return for helping someone."

"I say," Peter said, musingly, "wouldn't it be fun if we all were in a book, and you were writing it?

Then you could make all sorts of jolly things happen, and make Jim's legs get well at once and be all right tomorrow; and make father come home soon and—"

"Do you miss your father very much?" mother asked.

Peter thought she spoke rather coldly.

"Awfully," Peter replied, briefly.

Mother was enveloping and addressing the second letter.

"You see," Peter went on slowly, "you see, it's not just about missing father, but with him being away there's no other man in the house except me. That's why I want Jim to stay so much. It would be so nice if you could write such a book and make daddy come home soon!"

Peter's mother put her arm round him suddenly, and hugged him in silence for a minute.

Then she said, "Don't you think it's rather nice that we're in a book that God is writing? If I were writing the book, I might make mistakes. But God knows how to make the story end just right in the way that's best for us all."

** ** ** ** ** ** ** ** **

It was soon after breakfast that a knock came at the door. The children were busy cleaning the brass candlesticks in honor of Jim's visit. They had managed to get all grubby and disheveled.

"That'll be the doctor," mother said, "I'll go. Shut the kitchen door and for heaven's sake do not come out. You're not fit to be seen."

It wasn't the doctor. They knew that by the voice and also by the sound of the boots that went upstairs. They did not recognize the sound of the boots, but everyone was certain that they had heard the voice before. There was a long interval.

'Who can it possibly be?' they kept on asking themselves and each other.

"Listen—the door's opening. Now they'll come down. I'll open the door a crack," Peter said.

"Bobbie," they heard mother call. They opened the kitchen door, and mother leaned over the stair railing.

"Jim's grandfather has come," she said. "Wash your hands and faces, then come up and meet him. He wants to see you!"

The bedroom door shut again.

"Let's have some hot water, Mrs. Viney. I'm as black as your hat," Peter said.

The three were indeed dirty. They were still busy with soap and flannel, when they heard the boots and the voice come down the stairs and go into the dining room. Once they were clean, they went into the dining room. Mother was sitting in the window seat, and in the leather-covered armchair that father always used to sit in before, sat their 'own old gentleman!'

"Well, I never!" Peter said, even before he wished, "How do you do?"

"It's our own old gentleman!" Phyllis cried.

"Oh, it's you!" Bobbie exclaimed.

And then they remembered themselves and their manners and said, "How do you do?" very nicely.

"This is Jim's grandfather," mother said.

"How splendid!" Peter said with excitement. "That's just exactly like a book, isn't it, mother?"

"It is, rather," mother said smiling. "Things do happen in real life that are rather like books sometimes."

"I hope," Peter said, "you're not going to take Jim away, though, are you?"

"Not at present," the old gentleman said. "Your mother has most kindly consented to let him stay here. I thought of sending a nurse, but your mother is good enough to say that she will nurse him herself."

"But what about her writing?" Peter said, before anyone could stop him. "There won't be anything for him to eat if mother doesn't write."

"That's all right," mother said, hastily.

The old gentleman looked very kindly at mother.

"Your mother, my dears, has consented to give up writing for a little while and to become matron of my hospital."

"Oh!" Phyllis said, blankly. "And shall we have to go away from Three Chimneys and the railway and everything?"

"No, no, darling," mother said, hurriedly.

"The hospital is called Three Chimneys Hospital," the old gentleman said, "and my unlucky Jim is the only patient, and I hope he'll continue to be so. Your mother will be matron, and there'll be a hospital staff of a housemaid and a cook, till Jim's well."

"And then so, will mother go on writing again?" asked Peter.

"We shall see," the old gentleman said, with a slight, swift glance at Bobbie, "perhaps something nice may happen and she won't have to. One never knows."

The old gentleman rose to leave.

"I'm so glad," Peter said, "that you're going to keep him, mother."

"Take care of your mother, my dears. She's one in a million. God bless her," the old gentleman said, taking both mother's hands, "God bless her! Dear me, where's my hat? Bobbie will you come with me to the gate?"

At the gate he stopped and said, "You're a good child, my dear. I got your letter but it wasn't needed. I had read about your father's case in the papers, when it happened. At that time itself I had my doubts. And ever since I've known who you were, I've been trying to find out things. I haven't done very much yet. But I have hopes, my dear, I have hopes."

"Oh!" Bobbie said, choking a little. "I know you can do it. You don't think father did it, do you?"

"My dear," he said, "I'm perfectly certain he did not."

CHAPTER 15

The End

Life at the Three Chimneys changed a lot after the old gentleman came to see his grandson. The cook, Clara and the housemaid, Ethelwyn were very nice, but they told mother they did not seem to want Mrs. Viney. So, Mrs. Viney came only two days a week to do washing and ironing. They even asked the children not to interfere with their work. This left the children with a lot of free time. At the same time mother had no writing to do now, so it meant she had time for their lessons. Though mother was nice, their lessons never became as interesting as peeling potatoes or lighting a fire. On the other hand, if mother now had time for lessons, she also had time for play, and to make up little rhymes for the children as she used to do.

There was one very odd thing about these lessons. Whatever the children did, they always wanted to do something else. When Peter was doing his Latin, he thought it would be nice to be learning history like Bobbie. Bobbie would have preferred arithmetic, which was what Phyllis happened to be doing, and Phyllis of course thought Latin was the most interesting kind of lesson. And so on.

Then slowly, as Jim's leg got better, it was very

pleasant to go up and sit with him and hear tales about his school life and the other boys. Peter listened to all this with immense pleasure.

Mother wrote a poem for Jim also. Jim could never understand how mother could have been clever enough to do it. To the others it seemed nice, but natural. Jim taught Peter to play chess and draughts and dominoes, and altogether it was a wonderful time.

As Jim's leg got better, Bobbie and Phil thought that they should do something different. They racked their brains but couldn't think of anything.

"Things do happen by themselves sometimes, without you making them," Phyllis said, as though everything that happened in the world was her doing.

"I wish something would happen, something wonderful," Bobbie said, dreamily.

And something wonderful did happen exactly four days after she had said this.

They seemed to be hardly 'railway children' at all

those days, and as the days went on, each had an uneasy feeling about this, which Phyllis expressed one day.

"I wonder if the railway misses us!" she said, sadly. "We never go to see it now."

"It seems ungrateful," Bobbie said. "We loved it so much when we hadn't anyone else to play with."

"The thing I don't like," Bobbie said, "is our having stopped waving to the 9.15 and sending our love to father by it."

"Let's begin it again," Phyllis said.

And they did.

It was September now, and the grass on the slope to the railway was dry and crisp.

"Hurry up," Peter said, "or we shall miss the 9.15!"

"I can't hurry more than I am doing," Phyllis said. "Oh! My bootlace has come undone again!"

"Even when you're getting married," Peter said, "your bootlace will come undone while going up the church aisle. The man you're going to get married to, will tumble over it and smash his nose in. Then you'll say you won't marry him, and you'll have to be an old maid."

"I won't," Phyllis said tartly. "I'd much rather marry a man with his nose smashed in than not marry anybody."

"Look! The signal's down. We must run!" cried Peter.

They ran. And once more they waved their handkerchiefs, without at all minding whether the handkerchiefs were clean or not, to the 9.15.

"Take our love to father!" cried Bobbie.

And the others, too, shouted, "Take our love to father!"

The old gentleman waved quite violently from his first-class carriage window. And there was nothing odd in that, for he had always waved. But what was really remarkable was that from every window, handkerchiefs fluttered, newspapers signaled and hands waved wildly. The train swept by with a rustle and roar, the little pebbles jumped and danced under it as it passed, and the children were left looking at each other.

"Well!" Peter said.

"Well!" Bobbie said.

"Well!" Phyllis said.

"What on earth does that mean?" asked Peter, but he did not expect any answer.

"I don't know," Bobbie said.

"Perhaps the old gentleman told the people at his station to look out for us and wave. He knew we would like it!"

Somehow, unknowingly, Peter was very right. This was just what had happened. The old gentleman, who was very well known and respected at his particular station, had got there early that morning. He had waited at the door and said something to every single passenger who passed through that door. And after nodding to what the old gentleman had said, each passenger had gone onto the platform and read one certain part of his newspaper. When the passengers got into the train, they told the other passengers who were already there, what the old gentleman had said, and then the other passengers had also looked at their newspapers and seemed astonished and also pleased. Then, when the train passed the fence where the three children were standing, newspapers, hands and handkerchiefs were waved madly.

"I think they were trying to explain something to us with the newspapers," said Bobbie.

"Explain what?" asked Peter, not unnaturally.

"I don't know," Bobbie answered, "but I do feel most awfully funny. I feel as if something is going to happen."

Once they were home, they sat for their lessons. Today Bobbie found it even more difficult to pay attention to her lessons. Mother looked at her anxiously.

"Are you not well, dear?" she asked.

"I don't know how I feel. It isn't that I'm lazy. Mother, will you let me off lessons today? I just want to be alone by myself."

"Yes, of course I'll let you off," mother said. "But what is it, my sweetheart? You don't feel ill, do you?"

"I don't know," Bobbie answered, a little breathlessly, "but I want to be by myself and see why my head feels all silly and my inside all squirmy-twisty. I think I would feel better in the garden," Bobbie said.

She could not stay in the garden either. It was one of those shiny autumn days, when everything does seem to be waiting. Bobbie could not wait.

'I'll go down to the station,' she thought, 'talk to Perks and ask about the signalman's little boy.'

So she went down. On the way she passed the old lady from the post-office, who gave her a kiss and a hug; and the draper's boy, who was usually not so civil, touched his cap, and said, 'Morning, miss.'

"Oh!" Bobbie said to herself, and her heart quickened its beats. "Something is going to happen!"

The stationmaster wrung her hand warmly. But he gave her no reason for this unusually enthusiastic greeting.

He only said, "The 11.54's a bit late, miss," and went away very quickly into his office.

Perks did not appear until the 11.54 was signaled, and he, like everybody else that morning, had a newspaper in his hand.

"Hello!" he said. "Here you are. Well, if this is the train, it'll be smart work! Well, God bless you, my dear! I saw it in the paper, and I don't think I was ever so glad of anything!"

"Saw what in the paper?" asked Bobbie, but already the 11.54 was steaming into the station, and the stationmaster was looking at all the places where Perks was not and ought to have been. Bobbie was left standing alone, the station cat watching her from under the bench with friendly golden eyes.

Only three people got out of the 11.54. The first was a countryman with two baskets and a box full of live chickens; the second was Miss Peckitt, the grocer's wife's cousin, with a tin box and three brown-paper parcels and the third—

"Oh! My daddy, my daddy!"

That scream went like a knife into the heart of everyone in the train, and people put their heads out of the windows to see a tall pale man with lips set in a thin close line, and a little girl clinging to him with arms and legs, while his arms went tightly round her.

** ** ** ** ** ** ** ** **

"I knew something wonderful was going to happen," Bobbie said, as they went up the road, "but I didn't think it was going to be this. Oh, daddy, my daddy!"

"Then didn't mother get my letter?" father asked.

"There weren't any letters this morning."

"You must go in by yourself, Bobbie, and tell mother quietly that it's all right. They've caught the man who did it. Everyone knows now that it wasn't your daddy."

"I always knew it wasn't you," Bobbie said. "Mother and our old gentleman too said that you did not do it."

"Yes," he said, "it's all 'his' doing. Mother wrote and told me you had discovered what was going on. And she told me what a pillar of support you had been to her. My own little girl!"

They stopped a minute then.

And now I see them crossing the field. Bobbie goes into the house, trying to keep her eyes from speaking before her lips have found the right words to tell mother quietly that father has come home.' Father stands outside the nearest door. Now the house door opens. Bobbie's voice calls, 'Come in, daddy come in!' He goes in and the door is shut.

And so Peter, Phil and Bobbie had their family together once again. It was just as mother had said; 'God knows how to make the story end perfectly, in the way that's best for us all.'

THE END